THIS BOOK BELONGS TO:

Anna Sewell

was born in 1820. She wrote
many stories and poems for children,
but *Black Beauty*, published when she
was 57 years old, is her only novel.
She dedicated it to her mother,
Mary Wright Sewell, who was also
a popular children's author.

———————

Jonathan Mercer's woodcuts have been made
specially for Ladybird Classics. They are individually
hand-crafted from box-wood.

Ladybird

A catalogue record for this book is available from the British Library

Published by Ladybird Books Ltd
80 Strand London WC2R 0RL
A Penguin Company

10

© LADYBIRD BOOKS LTD MCMXCIV

LADYBIRD CLASSICS

BLACK BEAUTY

by Anna Sewell

Retold by Betty Evans and Audrey Daly
Illustrated by David Barnett
Woodcuts by Jonathan Mercer

'I hope you will grow up gentle and good...'

MY EARLY HOME

The very first place that I can remember was a large pleasant meadow. To start with, I lived on my mother's milk. But as soon as I could eat grass, she had to go out to work, and she came home in the evening.

There were six young colts in the meadow besides me. We had great fun galloping around, although they would sometimes bite and kick.

One day, my mother whinnied to me to come to her. Then she said, 'The colts who live here are very good colts. But they are carthorse colts, and, of course, they have not learned manners.

'I hope you will grow up gentle and good and never learn bad ways. Do your work as well as you can, and never bite or kick, even just in play.'

My mother was a wise old horse, and I have never forgotten her advice. Her name was Duchess, but our master often called her Pet.

As I grew older, I grew handsome. I had one white foot and a pretty white star on my forehead. My black coat grew fine and soft.

When I was four years old, Squire Gordon came to look at me. He seemed to like me, and said, 'When he has been broken in, he will do very well.' My master said he would break me in himself so that I would not be frightened or hurt.

Breaking in means to teach a horse to wear a saddle and bridle and to carry someone safely on his back. He must also learn to pull a carriage or cart, going fast or slow, just as his driver wishes. He has to learn never to bite or kick, nor to jump at anything he sees.

Even with a good master like mine, it was slow work, but at last it was done.

Next came iron shoes. That was frightening,

but the blacksmith did not hurt me, even when he drove nails through the shoe right into my hoof. My feet seemed stiff and heavy afterwards, but in time I got used to that.

Now that I was ready to leave home, my mother said to me, 'I hope you will fall into good hands, but a horse never knows who may buy him, or who may drive him. Some men are kind and thoughtful, like our master. Others can be cruel. Remember, do your best whatever happens, and keep up your good name.'

In the stall next to me was a pony called Merrylegs

BIRTWICK PARK

Early in May a man came from Squire Gordon's to take me away. I was taken into a big stable which had four good stalls and a swinging window that opened into the yard.

In the next stall to me was a pony called Merrylegs, whom the children used to ride. He was a favourite with everyone, and he and I soon became great friends.

There was a stable boy called James Howard, and the coachman's name was John Manly. He had a wife and one little child, and they lived in the coachman's cottage, very near to the stables.

The next day I was taken to my new master, so that he could try me out. I found that Squire Gordon was a very good rider, and kind to his horse as well. When we came home, his lady was at the Hall door to greet us.

'Well, my dear,' she said, 'how do you like him?'

'He has a fine spirit,' my master replied. 'What shall we call him?'

She looked up at me. 'He really is a beauty, and he has such a sweet good-tempered face and such a fine intelligent eye – how about "Black Beauty"?'

'Black Beauty – why yes, that shall be his name.' And so it was.

Also in our stable was a chestnut mare called Ginger. Although she was rather bad-tempered, we grew quite friendly. Sometimes we went out together in double harness, and then we talked to each other. She wanted to know all about my early life, and I told her.

Then she told me about her life, and it was very different from mine. No one had ever been kind to Ginger.

After she had been broken in, she was sent to London to a fashionable gentleman, as one of a matching pair. 'There I was driven with a bearing rein,' she said, 'and I really hated it. I like to toss my head about and hold it as high as any horse. But just imagine, if you tossed your head up high and had to hold it there for hours on end! That's what happens with a bearing rein.

'I grew more and more irritable. One day, just as they were straining my head up with that rein, I began to plunge and kick with all my might. That was the end of that place! I was sold and went back to the country. Alas, the groom at the new place was rough, so I bit him. I was sold again and came here not long before you did. It's better here, of course, but for how long?'

As it turned out, kindness was all Ginger needed. Her bad temper slowly died and she became quite gentle and happy at Birtwick Park.

A big tree crashed to the ground

A STORMY DAY

One late autumn day, my master and John had to go on a long journey on business. I was put into the dogcart, which I always enjoyed.

We went along merrily until we came to a low wooden bridge. The river banks were rather high, and the bridge, instead of rising in the middle, went across straight and level. That meant that if the river was full, the water would be nearly up to the wooden planks.

Master had to pay at the tollgate before we could cross. The man there said the river was rising fast, and he feared it would be a bad night.

We started for home late in the afternoon. By then the wind was blowing so hard that a big tree crashed to the ground beside the road. I heard

13

the master say to John that he had never been out in such a storm.

It was very nearly dark by the time we got back to the bridge. We could just see that the water was over the middle of it, but as that happened sometimes when the river was high, Master did not stop. We were going along at a good pace, but the moment my feet touched the first part of the bridge, I knew there was something wrong. I did not dare to go forward, so I stopped dead.

'There's something wrong, sir,' said John. He sprang out of the dogcart and tried to lead me forward. 'Come on, Beauty, what's the matter?'

Just then the man at the tollgate on the other side ran out of the house, waving a torch about and shouting at the top of his voice. 'What's the matter?' shouted my master.

'The bridge is broken in the middle and part of it is carried away. You can't cross.'

'Thank God!' said my master.

'You Beauty!' said John, and took the bridle and gently turned me round to the right-hand road by the riverside. The next bridge was much further up the river, and we had a long way to go.

At last we came home to the Hall. As we came up, Mistress ran out, saying, 'Are you really safe, my dear? Oh! I have been so anxious. Have you had an accident?'

'No, my dear, but if your Black Beauty had not been wiser than we were, we should all have been carried down the river at the wooden bridge.'

Then John took me to the stable. Oh, what a fine supper he gave me that night – a good bran mash and some crushed beans with my oats – and such a thick bed of straw! I was glad of it, for I was tired.

We stopped at a big hotel in the Market Place

THE FIRE

My master and mistress decided one day to visit some friends who lived about fifty miles away. James Howard, the stable boy, was to drive them. He was leaving us shortly to go to a better job, and needed the practice in driving. The first day we travelled thirty two miles. There were long heavy hills, but James drove so carefully that Ginger and I were not at all harassed.

Just as the sun was going down, we reached the town where we were to spend the night. We stopped at a big hotel in the Market Place. We drove into a long yard, and two ostlers came to take us to our stalls in a long stable.

Later on in the evening, a traveller's horse was brought in by one of the ostlers. While the ostler was grooming, a young man with a pipe in his mouth came into the stable for a gossip.

'I say, Towler,' said the ostler, 'run up into the loft and put some hay down into this horse's rack, will you? Only put your pipe down first!'

'All right,' said the other. A few moments later I heard him step across the floor overhead and put down the hay. Then James came in for a last look at us before he went to bed. When he left, the door was locked and we were left alone.

I don't know what time of night it was, but I woke up feeling very uncomfortable. The stable seemed full of smoke and I could hardly breathe.

I heard Ginger coughing, and the other horses seemed restless, pulling at their halters, and many of them were stamping.

I heard a soft rushing noise, and a low crackling. There was something so strange about it that it made me tremble all over.

At last Dick Towler burst in with a lantern and

began to untie the horses, to lead them out. He seemed so frightened himself that he frightened us as well, and none of us would go with him. He tried us all in turn, then left the stable.

I saw a red light flickering on the wall, and heard a roaring noise. Then there was a cry of 'Fire'.

The next thing I heard was James's voice, quiet and cheery, as it always was. 'Come on, Beauty, we'll soon be out of here.' He took the scarf off his neck and tied it lightly over my eyes, and, patting and coaxing, he led me out of the stable. When we were safe in the yard, he slipped the scarf off my eyes and shouted, 'Here, somebody! Take this horse while I go back for another.'

A tall, broad man stepped forward and took me, and James ran back into the stable. I set up a shrill whinny as I saw him go. Ginger told me afterwards that whinny was the best thing I could have done for her. Had she not heard me, she would never have had the courage to come out.

There was much confusion in the yard as the horses were brought out of other stables. I kept my eye fixed on the stable door, where the smoke poured out thicker than ever, and I could see flashes of red light.

Then I gave a joyful neigh – James was coming through the smoke, leading Ginger, who was coughing violently. Suddenly there came a sound of galloping feet and loud rumbling wheels. Two horses dashed into the yard pulling a heavy fire engine, and the firemen leapt to the ground. The flames rose in a great blaze from the roof.

Next day, everyone was wondering how the fire had started. At last an ostler remembered that Dick Towler had been smoking a pipe when he came into the stable. Dick said that he had put his pipe down, but no one believed him. Pipes were never allowed in the stable at Birtwick Park, and I thought it ought to be the rule everywhere.

The firemen leapt to the ground

JOE GREEN

After that terrible night, it was good to get home to Birtwick Park. John was equally glad to see us, and had a good deal of praise for the courage James had shown at the fire.

Before he and James left us for the night, James said, 'Who is coming in my place?'

'Little Joe Green at the Lodge,' said John. 'He is small, but he is quick, and willing and kindhearted as well.'

The next day Joe came to the stables to learn all he could before James left. He learned to sweep the stable and bring in the new straw and hay. He began to clean the harness, and helped to wash the carriage. He was too small to groom Ginger and me, so James taught him on

Merrylegs. He was a nice little fellow, and always came whistling to his work.

Merrylegs was a good deal put out at being 'mauled about' as he said, 'by a boy who knew nothing.' Towards the end of the second week, however, he told me confidentially that he thought the boy would turn out well.

At last the day came when James had to leave us. He wasn't very happy about it, and he looked quite downhearted that morning.

John tried to cheer him up, but everyone was sorry to lose James.

We went like the wind

GOING FOR THE DOCTOR

Not long after James had left, I was awakened suddenly in the night by the stable bell ringing loudly. Then John came in, saying, 'Wake up, Beauty, you must go fast now, if ever you did. The mistress is ill and we must go for the doctor.'

We went like the wind, and the church clock struck three as we drew up at Doctor White's door. John knocked at the door like thunder. Doctor White put his head out of the window. 'What do you want?' he said.

'Mrs Gordon is very ill, sir. Master wants you to go at once. He thinks she will die if you cannot get there.'

Doctor White was soon at the door. 'The worst of it is,' he said, 'my horse has been out all day

25

and is quite worn out. What is to be done? Can I have your horse?'

'He has come at a gallop nearly all the way, sir, but I think my master would not be against it if you think fit, sir.'

'All right,' said the doctor. 'I will soon be ready.'

The way back seemed long, but I did my best.

I was glad to get home. My legs shook under me, and I could only stand and pant. I had not a dry hair on my body, the water ran down my legs, and I steamed all over.

For the next few days I was very ill, and Mr Bond the horse doctor came every day. John would get up two or three times in the night to come to me. My master often came to see me, too. 'My poor Beauty,' he said one day, 'you saved your mistress's life!' I was very glad to hear that, for it seems the doctor said that had we been a little longer it would have been too late.

I don't know how long I was ill, but I thought I was going to die, and I believe they all thought so, too.

When I grew well again, I found that sad changes were about to happen. We heard from time to time that our mistress was ill. Then we heard that she must go to a warm country for two or three years. The master began immediately to make arrangements for leaving England.

We used to hear it talked about in our stable; indeed, nothing else was talked about. John went about his work silent and sad, and Joe scarcely whistled.

At last the day came when we took our master and mistress to the station. As the train glided away, John sighed. 'We shall never see her again,' he said. 'Never.' He took the reins, mounted the box and, with Joe, drove slowly home – but it would not be home to us from now on.

John came round to each of us

EARLSHALL

Next morning Joe took Merrylegs to the vicarage, for he had been given to the vicar. Then John took Ginger and me to Earlshall Park, where we were to live.

A groom took us to a light, airy stable. In a short while John and our new coachman, Mr York, came in to see us. John said, 'I had better mention that we have never used the bearing rein with either of these horses.'

'If they come here,' said York, 'they will have to wear the bearing rein. My lady has to have style, and her carriage horses must be reined up tight.'

Then John came round to each of us to pat and speak to us for the last time. His voice sounded very sad. I never saw him again.

Next afternoon we took my lady for a drive. When she came out, she said, 'York, put those horses' heads higher – they're not fit to be seen.'

York got down and shortened the bearing rein by one hole, and I began to understand what I had heard. It made it much harder to pull uphill.

As the days went by, the rein grew really short. I was very unhappy, but Ginger really hated it. One dreadful day came when she kicked York's hat off and reared so much that she fell down.

After this, Ginger was used for hunting and was never put into a carriage again.

I was given a new partner called Max, but we still had to suffer the tight rein. In my old home, I always knew that John and my master were my friends. Here at Earlshall, although I was quite well treated, I had no friend. York never tried to help over that rein. Time went on, and I grew tired and depressed, hating my work. But sadly, much worse was to come.

REUBEN SMITH'S
DOWNFALL

When our master and his family went to London in the spring, they left Reuben Smith in charge of the horses that stayed behind. He was a very good man – most of the time. He had one great fault, however – the love of drink, although he had promised never to touch another drop.

Just before the family was due to return, Smith had to go up to town, and he chose me for the journey. On the way there, he was his usual thoughtful self.

In town, however, he began to drink, and it was late when we started back. Suddenly he began to gallop, harder and harder. Sometimes he whipped me, although I was already going at full speed. I had a loose shoe, and the speed we were going at loosened it still more. It came off and I stumbled, falling on my knees. Smith was flung off by my fall and lay groaning some distance away. After a while, he stopped groaning and lay still.

At first it was thought that Reuben Smith's death was my fault. Then my sore hoof was discovered, and everyone realised that Smith must have been drinking. Later, several people said that he had been drunk when we left town.

As soon as my knees were more or less healed, I was turned into a small meadow for a month or two. Ginger was there too, and we were glad to see each other.

She said that she had been ruined by hard riding and they were going to see if rest would help. We both felt that we were not what we had been.

One day the Earl came into the meadow with

Smith was flung off by my fall

York. The Earl seemed very annoyed as they looked us over. 'What makes me most angry,' he said, 'is that these horses of my old friend, who thought they would find a good home with me, are ruined. The black one will have to be sold: I can't have knees like that in my stables. See if you can find him a good home.'

And about a week later, I was bought by the master of some livery stables, and left Earlshall. I had become a job horse, which meant that I could be hired out to anyone who wished to drive me.

LIFE AS A JOB HORSE

Some of the people who wanted to hire me couldn't drive at all. As I was good-tempered and gentle, I think I was more often let out to the bad drivers than some of the others, because I could be depended upon.

Of course, we sometimes came in for good driving. One morning I was put into a light gig and taken to a house in Pulteney Street. Two gentlemen came out. The taller of them took the reins, and I can remember even now how quietly he turned me round. Then, with a light feel of the rein and drawing the whip gently across my back, we were off.

I arched my neck and set off at my best pace because I had someone behind me who knew how

Filcher… groomed me thoroughly

a good horse ought to be driven. It seemed like old times again!

This gentleman took a great liking to me, and eventually I was sold to a friend of his, Mr Barry, who wanted a safe, pleasant horse for riding. I had yet another new master.

At first this seemed a good change. My groom, a man called Filcher, had once been an ostler at a hotel, but now he grew fruit and vegetables for the market. His wife bred chickens and rabbits for sale.

Filcher kept the stable clean and airy, and he groomed me thoroughly. He was never otherwise than gentle, and he certainly knew his job.

When I first went there, I heard the master give the order for food – the best hay, with oats and beans, and bran with rye grass, as Filcher thought necessary. I was going to be well off!

After a while, however, I found I wasn't getting anything like the amount of oats I should have had. I grew tired and unhappy.

A farmer friend of Mr Barry's noticed this one day. He looked me over more carefully. Then he said to my master, 'I don't know who gets the oats you pay for, but it certainly isn't your horse! I suggest you look into what's happening in your stable. Some scoundrels are mean enough to rob a dumb beast of his food.'

When Mr Barry took his advice, the police discovered that my oats were being fed to Mrs Filcher's rabbits! Had I been able to speak, I could have told him that. I had seen Filcher's little boy come every morning to collect the oats that his father stole.

Filcher went to prison for two months, and in a few days' time I had a new groom.

THE HUMBUG

Alfred Smirk was a tall, good-looking fellow, but if ever there was a humbug in the shape of a groom, he was that man. He was very civil to me, and never used me ill. In fact, he did a great deal of stroking and patting when his master was there to see it.

He thought himself very handsome and spent a lot of time in front of a little mirror in the harness room. Everyone thought he was a very nice young man, but I should say he was the laziest, most conceited fellow I ever came near.

Of course, it was wonderful not to be ill used, but a horse wants more than that. I had a loose box and might have been very comfortable if Smirk had not been too lazy to clean it out and take the damp straw away. As to cleaning my feet or grooming me properly, he never did those things at all. Standing on damp straw had made my feet grow tender and unhealthy. When I stumbled twice in an afternoon, my master took me to the farrier to see what was wrong.

'Your horse has got the thrush, badly,' said the farrier. 'His feet are very tender. We find this sort of thing in dirty stables where the litter isn't cleaned out.'

He cleaned and treated each hoof in turn, and then he ordered all the litter to be taken out of my box day by day and the floor kept very clean.

My feet were soon all right again. Mr Barry, however, was so much disgusted at being twice deceived by his grooms that he decided to give up keeping a horse altogether.

I was sold again – this time into a very different kind of life. My new master was a cab driver called Jeremiah Barker, usually known as Jerry.

'His feet are very tender'

A LONDON CAB HORSE

That first evening, I knew I was going to be happy there. Jerry's wife, Polly, came to see me, along with their eight-year-old daughter, Dolly. Their son, Harry, who was twelve, had already been helping to groom me and their other horse, Captain.

Polly and her little girl made much of me, and it was a great treat to be petted again, and talked to in a gentle voice.

Polly thought I was very handsome and much too good to be a cab horse, if it were not for my broken knees. 'We don't know whose fault that was,' said Jerry. 'I shall give him the benefit of the doubt, for I never drove a firmer, neater stepper.'

The first week of my life as a cab horse was very trying. I was anxious and harassed by the noise and the hurry of London traffic. But Jerry was a good driver, and he took as much thought for his horses as he did for himself. He kept us very clean, and always fed us well.

But the best thing about my time there was our Sundays for rest. One lady wanted us to take her to church every Sunday, but Jerry said working seven days a week was too much for his horses as well as himself. The lady was quite cross at first, but then she saw that he was right. Jerry didn't lose her custom over it.

Christmas and the New Year are very merry times for some people. But for cabmen and their horses it is no holiday. There are so many parties and balls that the work is hard and often late. Sometimes driver and horse have to wait for hours, shivering with cold, while the cheery people inside are dancing away to the music.

We had a great deal of late work in Christmas week. Jerry had a bad cough, and standing around in the cold made it worse. One night when we got home it was so bad that he couldn't speak. He gave me a rubdown as usual, although he could hardly get his breath. Then Polly brought me a warm meal, and they locked the door for the night.

Next day was very strange. Harry came in to clean and feed us, and to sweep out the stalls, but he didn't whistle or sing as he usually did.

Two days passed like that, and there was great trouble indoors, because Jerry was dangerously ill.

He grew better at last, but the doctor said that he must never go back to the cab work again.

After a while, Jerry managed to find a job as a coachman. A cottage with a garden went with the job, and the family was very pleased.

As for me, I was heavy hearted as I was led away to a sale once more.

Polly brought me a warm meal

FARMER THOROUGHGOOD AND HIS GRANDSON

As I waited unhappily at the sale, I noticed a man who looked like a gentleman farmer. I saw his eye rest on me, and I pricked my ears and looked at him.

'There's a horse, Willie, that has known better days,' he said to a young boy with him. He gave me a kind pat as he spoke.

'Poor old fellow! Couldn't you buy him and make him strong again, Grandpapa?' asked the boy, stroking my face. 'Just like you did with Ladybird?'

The farmer laughed. 'I can't buy every old horse and make him strong again.' As he spoke,

46

he slowly felt my legs. 'Just trot him out, will you?' he said to the man who had brought me.

I arched my poor thin neck, raised my tail a little and threw out my legs as well as I could, for they were very stiff.

'All right, I'll take him,' said the farmer, whose name was Mr Thoroughgood.

From then on, I had good food, perfect rest, soft turf and gentle exercise. I began to feel quite young again!

One day in March, Mr Thoroughgood tried me out in the light carriage. My legs were no longer stiff, and I did the work with perfect ease.

Mr Thoroughgood was pleased. He said to Willie, 'Now we must look for a quiet place for him, where he will be well looked after.'

One day that summer, the groom cleaned and brushed me with such care that I thought some new change must be at hand. I think even the harness had an extra polish.

Willie seemed half-anxious, half-merry, as he got into the carriage with his grandfather. 'If the ladies take to him,' said the old gentleman, 'they'll be suited and he'll be suited. We can but try.'

We drove through the village and up to a pretty house with a lawn and shrubbery at the front. Willie stayed with me while Mr Thoroughgood went into the house. Soon he returned, followed by three ladies.

They all came and looked at me and asked questions. One lady took to me greatly. She said she was sure she should like me, I had such a good face. Another – a tall, pale lady – said that she would always be nervous in riding behind a horse that had once been down. 'It isn't always the horse's fault,' said Mr Thoroughgood. 'Why don't you have him on trial for a while, so that your coachman can see what he thinks?'

And so it was arranged. In the morning the

They all came and looked at me

ladies' smart-looking groom came for me.
I was led home, placed in a comfortable stable,
fed, and left to myself.

The next day, when the groom was cleaning my
face, he said, 'That is just like the star that Black
Beauty had.'

He went on talking to himself. 'He was much
the same height, too. I wonder where he is now.'

Then he noticed my white foot and began to
look me over more carefully. 'White star on the
forehead, one white foot on the off-side.'

Then, looking at my back, 'And there is that
little patch of white that we used to call
"Beauty's threepenny bit". It *must* be Black
Beauty! Why, Beauty! Beauty! Do you remember
me – little Joe Green?' And he began patting and
patting me as if he was quite overjoyed.

That afternoon, after I had taken the ladies
for a safe gentle drive, I heard Joe telling them
that he was sure I was Squire Gordon's old Black

Beauty. They were already pleased with me, so they decided to keep me and call me by my old name of 'Black Beauty'.

I have now lived in this happy place a whole year. Joe is the best and kindest of grooms, and my work is easy and pleasant. My ladies have promised that I shall never be sold, so I have nothing to fear; and here my story ends.

My troubles are all over, and I am at home. Often before I am quite awake, I fancy I am still in the orchard at Birtwick, standing with my old friends under the apple trees.